NODDY™

Cheer Up, Little Noddy!

HarperCollins *Children's Books*

It was a beautiful day in Toyland and the birds were singing. Noddy was waxing his little red and yellow car, nodding his head as he did so. He gave the headlights one last rub with his cloth and stepped back to admire his work. "Ah," he said with a satisfied sigh, "I do love you, little car."

"Parp-parp," replied the car.

Yes, Noddy was feeling very happy, but that was all about to change…

"Your car does look beautiful today, Noddy," chirped a cheeky voice. It was Master Tubby Bear.

"I've just spent all day cleaning and scrubbing and washing and waxing it," said Noddy, "so it should look beautiful!"

"Let me have a drive, Noddy, oh please!" begged the bear.

Noddy would never be foolish enough to let Tubby Bear drive his car, but he did feel so happy on this particular day that he decided to allow his friend to just sit in the car for a while.

Master Tubby Bear was pleased.

"Oh, thank you, Noddy!

Straight away, he sat in the car and started bouncing on the newly dusted seats and honking the newly polished horn.

"Oh, do be careful, Tubby," said Noddy as he went inside to start making his tea. Master Tubby Bear was being so noisy, Noddy could even hear the car's 'parp-parp' from the kitchen.

"Oh, shush," Noddy called out, and after a moment or two the 'parp-parp' got quieter and quieter until it was silent again.

"That's better," thought Noddy. But then he had a second thought. The sound of the car would only get quieter and quieter if...

Noddy rushed outside and, sure enough, his little red and yellow car, his pride and joy, was gone. Naughty Master Tubby Bear had driven off with it, even though Noddy had told him not to.

Noddy rushed through Toy Town, looking for Tubby Bear and his taxi. Suddenly, Big-Ears whizzed up on his bicycle. He looked very serious indeed.

"I think you had better come with me, Noddy," he said.

Soon Noddy was looking at his little red and yellow car again, but instead of sighing with joy, he was sighing with sadness. That mischievous Tubby Bear had crashed his beautiful taxi into a large oak tree. The bumper was still nice and shiny but it was also bent out of shape.

Mr Sparks the mechanic stepped out of his breakdown van, took one look and made a long whistling sound. "This is going to be a very, VERY big job," he said.

Tears formed in Noddy's eyes.

The tears were still there as Noddy sat down for tea at Big-Ears' house.

"That Master Tubby Bear is always causing trouble," said Big Ears. "I'm sure he's the person responsible for stealing my washing off the line and treading all over my flower beds."

"It was my mistake," said Noddy, with a sad lump in his throat. "I should never have left him alone with the car. Oh, Big-Ears, what I am to do? How can I earn the money for the repairs without my taxi?"

Big-Ears thought long and hard as he munched on a googleberry muffin. He found that muffins helped him think up good ideas. And, sure enough, one came to him.

"You must borrow a wheelbarrow, Noddy," said Big Ears, "and everyone will give you errands. You can fetch their shopping and deliver their mail and charge one coin for each journey. You will soon make enough to fix your taxi!"

Noddy felt much better. The next day he borrowed a wheelbarrow from Master Tubby Bear, who was very sorry for all the trouble he had caused.

Very soon everyone in Toy Town was asking Noddy to run errands for them.

"Can you pick up some bananas from the shop for me?" asked Martha Monkey.

"Could you take these heavy deliveries for me?" pleaded Dinah Doll.

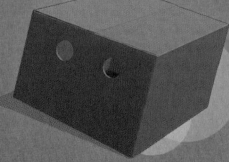

That tea-time, Noddy was back at Big-Ears'
house with Bumpy Dog. He was so exhausted
that he could barely speak and he fell asleep
in his friend's chair without eating so much
as one mouthful of his tea.

Big Ears felt a little guilty. He had told
everyone to give Noddy as many errands
as they could! Perhaps his good idea
hadn't been so good after all.

"**Neigh!**" Big-Ears jumped out of his chair.
That was the strange sound he kept hearing
every time someone stole his
washing and trampled over
his poor flowers. He quickly
ran out to his garden…

21

"Noddy, wake up! Look what I found to save the day." Noddy could hear his best friend, Big-Ears, but all he could see was the funny face of a horse.

"What a strange dream I am having," said Noddy.

"You're not dreaming, Noddy. I found a horse in my garden. He's been eating my washing and stomping on my flowers," said Big-Ears excitedly, "but he could help you with your errands and then you won't be so tired!"

Noddy was pleased. What a stroke of luck! He took the horse back to his house, but it was a bit too energetic and kept knocking things over.

"You can stay in my garage," said Noddy, "I used to have a little red and yellow car but now…" Noddy tried not to think about his car because it made him sad.

"This horse will save the day," he thought. "Tomorrow, I will be able to do twice as many errands."

The day began very well indeed. Noddy attached a cart to the horse and began to fill it with all the deliveries he was being paid to carry, when Bumpy Dog came bounding up.

Bumpy Dog was, as always, very excited, and so was the horse. Before long, the playful horse was chasing the bouncing dog through the streets at high speed, sending all the parcels and packages in the cart flying.

"Oh, dear! All of my customers will be cross," thought Noddy.

The next day, Noddy tried tying the parcels and packages directly to the horse. "This really is my last chance," he thought.

Just then, Mr Plod popped up out of nowhere.
"Well, I never. Little Noddy, a thief!" said
the policeman.

Noddy didn't understand, so Mr Plod
explained that the horse had been missing
from the farm for a week.

"But we found him in Big-Ears' garden,"
cried Noddy.

"Hmmm, I'll let you off this time,"
said Mr Plod taking the horse with him.

Noddy sat in the road sadly. How could
he afford to fix his car now? But then
he heard a familiar sound.

"Parp-parp!" His taxi! It was fixed!

"You looked after it so well,"
explained Mr Sparks, "I was
able to fix it very quickly
and surprisingly cheaply."

"Hooray!" said Noddy
who was so happy, he gave
his car a big kiss!

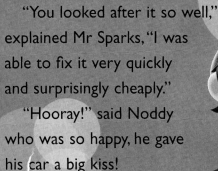

Read all of Noddy's Toyland Adventures!

Noddy Lends a Hand
ISBN 0 00 721069 8

Noddy's Unlucky Day
ISBN 0 00 721070 1

Noddy's Perfect Job
ISBN 0 00 721067 1

Busy Little Noddy
ISBN 0 00 721068 X

Noddy and Tessie Bear
ISBN 0 00 722345 5

Cheer Up, Little Noddy!
ISBN 0 00 722346 3

Noddy and Bumpy Dog
ISBN 0 00 722347 1

Noddy and the Aeroplane
ISBN 0 00 722348 X